Dog

Pig

Rat

牛
Ox

虎
Tiger

兔
Rabbit

Dragon

Snake

馬
Horse

羊
Sheep

猴
Monkey

雞
Rooster

For nearly 5,000 years, the Chinese culture has organized time in cycles of twelve years. This Eastern calendar is based upon the movement of the moon (as compared to the Western which follows the sun), and is symbolized by the zodiac circle. An animal that has unique qualities represents each year. Therefore, if you are born in a particular year, then you share the personality of that animal. Now people worldwide celebrate this two-week-long festival in the early spring and enjoy the start of another Chinese New Year.

To Amy and our two young pups, Lucas and Elias.
-O.C.

immedium
Immedium, Inc.
P.O. Box 31846
San Francisco, CA 94131
www.immedium.com

For information about special discounts for bulk purchases, please contact Immedium Special Sales at sales@immedium.com.

First hardcover edition (ISBN 978-1-59702-002-2) published 2006.

Edited by Don Menn
Book design by Elaine Chu and Dorothy Mak
Chinese translation by Ling Cho
Calligraphy by Lucy Chu

Printed in Malaysia
10 9 8 7 6 5 4 3 2 1

Library of Congress Cataloging-in-Publication Data

Names: Chin, Oliver Clyde, 1969- author. | Alcorn, Miah, illustrator.
Title: The year of the dog : tales from the Chinese zodiac / by Oliver Chin; illustrated by Jeremiah Alcorn.
Description: Revised edition. | San Francisco : Immedium, [2018] | Lists the birth years and characteristics of individuals born in the Chinese Year of the Dog. Includes bilingual translation in simplified Chinese | Summary: The adventures and misadventures of Daniel the puppy as he tries to learn how to be a loyal and dependable friend to the little girl who lives next door.
Identifiers: LCCN 2017012911 (print) | LCCN 2017021680 (ebook) | ISBN 9781597021401 (ebook) | ISBN 1597021407 (ebook) | ISBN 9781597021364 (hardback) | ISBN 1597021369
Subjects: | CYAC: Dogs--Fiction. | Animals--Infancy--Fiction. | Human-animal relationships--Fiction. | Astrology, Chinese--Fiction. | BISAC: JUVENILE FICTION / Holidays & Celebrations / Other, Non-Religious.
Classification: LCC PZ7.C44235 (ebook) | LCC PZ7.C44235 Yd 2018 (print) | DDC [E]--dc23
LC record available at https://lccn.loc.gov/2017012911

ISBN: 978-1-59702-136-4

The Year of the Dog

•Tales from the Chinese Zodiac•

十二生肖故事系列 狗年的故事

Written by Oliver Chin
Illustrated by Miah Alcorn

文： 陈曜豪
图： 艾尔康祖曼亚

www.immedium.com
San Francisco. CA

On New Year's Day, loud barking came from the doghouse.

Papa dog ran out and joyfully exclaimed, "It's time to celebrate!"

新年那天，狗屋里传出了高声吠叫。

狗爸爸从屋里跑出来，兴高彩烈的说："是时候庆祝了！"

Mama dog had just given birth to a bouncing baby pup.

“Let’s name him Daniel,” smiled Mama, and Papa agreed.

原来狗妈妈刚刚诞下了活泼的狗宝宝。

狗妈妈微笑着说：“就为他起名为丹尼尔吧！”
狗爸爸也同意用这个名字。

Later a girl visited and kissed Daniel hello.

After she departed, Daniel asked, **"Who was that?"**

过了些日子，一个小女孩来探望丹尼尔，并亲亲他表示问候。

当她离去后，丹尼尔就问："她是谁呀？"

Papa replied, “Lin is our neighbor and part of our family, too.”

狗爸爸答说：“莲是我们的邻居，
也是我们家庭的一份子。”

“She is very eager to play with you,” added Mama.

“她非常期待与你一起玩耍呢！”妈妈更补充说。

Since Daniel was a lively and curious puppy, he and Lin became fast friends.

Soon the two traveled everywhere together.

因为丹尼尔是一只充满活力和好奇的小狗，他和莲很快便成为好朋友。

不久，他们俩更一起四处旅遊。

They loved to explore the nearby fields and frolic in the streams.

他们爱往附近的田间探险，
也喜欢在溪涧里嬉戏。

Daniel barked happily at everything that crossed their path.

丹尼尔在旅行途中遇见任何事物
都会欢欣地叫嚷。

At home Mama said, “We are glad you and Lin get along so well.
Dogs and people are best friends, because we care for each other.”

妈妈常在家里说，“见到你和莲相处愉快，我们也感到欣慰，
因为我们互相关怀，所以狗和人类都成为好朋友。”

"Remember Daniel, you must always look after Lin," said Papa.

"Be ready to watch out for strangers wherever you are."

“记着，丹尼尔，你一定要时常照顾莲。”爸爸嘱咐他：
“无论你们在哪里都要对陌生人提高警觉！”

Papa described fantastic creatures that Daniel might meet someday.

The fiery Phoenix flew high with dazzling wings.

狗爸爸把丹尼尔将来可能会遇见的各种奇异动物都形容给他听。

火红的凤凰会拍着一对闪烁的翅膀高飞。

The sly dragon slithered with a long nose and a winding tail.

诡秘的龙带着他那长长的鼻子和弯弯曲曲的尾巴滑翔着。

And the ferocious tiger roared, flashing his bright stripes and sharp teeth.

还有那凶猛的老虎，会张开一副利牙和亮着一身虎纹嘶吼。

Amazed by Papa's tales, Daniel promised, **"I will do my best to protect Lin."**

听了爸爸的故事，丹尼尔不禁叹为观止，他于是答应说："我一定会尽全力保护莲的。"

Then one morning, a loud crowing awoke Daniel.

He gazed outside and saw a colorful bird flying onto the roof of Lin's house.

之后有一个早上，丹尼尔被咯咯的叫声吵醒。

他凝望窗外，看到一只彩雀飞上莲家的屋顶。

Sporting a blazing red crown and orange feathers, it approached Lin's bedroom window. Daniel thought it was the legendary phoenix and barked, **"Bow wow!"**

头上顶着鲜红的皇冠，身上披着橘橙的羽毛匆匆走着，见到彩雀走到莲房间的窗前，丹尼尔心里想着，这就是传说中的鳳凰吧！于是就"汪汪"地吠叫。

Lin heard Daniel's snarls and growls, and she opened her window.

听到丹尼尔的叫嚷、咆哮，
莲打开她的窗户查看。

"Oh, it is just a rooster," she yawned, and then went to get dressed.

"噢！那只不过是一只公鸡而已。"
她打了个呵欠就回去穿衣了。

Daniel whispered, **"I'm sorry I ruffled their feathers."**

丹尼尔轻声说："很对不起！我给他的羽毛惹急了。"

"Next time Daniel, don't be so hasty," suggested Mama.

"下次不要这么轻率，丹尼尔。"
妈妈提醒道。

Then one night, Daniel heard twigs cracking in the darkness.

又一个晚上，丹尼尔在黑暗中听到一枝桠断裂声 。

He peered outside and saw a shadow creeping near Lin's house.

他往外窥视，发现有一个黑影向莲的屋子慢慢靠近。

Waving its long tail, it poked its whiskered nose in the front door.

Daniel suspected it was the mythical dragon, and barked, **"Bow wow!"**

他摇着长尾巴，用长着胡须的鼻子一嗅一嗅地走向前门。

丹尼尔怀疑这就是神话中所说的那条龙，
他又禁不住汪汪地叫起来。

Opening the door,
Lin saw the creature
crawl into the moonlight.

打开门，莲见到有只动物在月光下爬行。

Lin sighed, "Oh, it is just a rat,"
and went back to sleep.

莲叹了一声，"噢！这只是一只老鼠。"
然后就回去睡觉。

Again, Daniel apologized,
"I'm sorry for disturbing everyone."

丹尼尔再次向她道歉：
"不好意思打扰了每一位休息。"

"Daniel, be more careful next time," warned Papa.

狗爸爸警告他："丹尼尔，你下次要更加小心才好。"

Daniel took his parents' advice to heart and didn't want to cause any more trouble.

丹尼尔把爸妈的忠告紧记在心，他不想再多惹麻烦了！

The dog held his tongue and tried to not bark when before he would have.

于是这只狗按捺着他的舌头，就算想吠的时候也尽量不去吠。

Nearby the pig, sheep, and horse liked the extra peace and quiet.

Daniel wanted to be patient and obedient, but it was very hard.

附近的猪、羊、和马等都喜欢这份额外的和平及宁静。

丹尼尔很想忍耐和听话，却觉得实在很难遵守。

One day, Mama and Papa told Daniel that they were going on a picnic.

"Lin and her parents are coming, so behave yourself," reminded Papa.

一天，狗爸爸和狗妈妈告诉丹尼尔他们要去野餐。

"莲和她的父母也一起去，所以你要好好检点呀！"
爸爸提点着。

They shared a hearty lunch in the forest, and then Lin wandered off by herself.

After a while, everyone wondered where Lin had gone.

他们在树林里享用了一顿丰富的午餐后，莲想自个儿蹓跶一下。

过了一会，人人都不知道莲去了哪里。

Daniel volunteered, **"I will fetch Lin!"** and dashed off to catch her scent.

Before long he spotted Lin walking in a grassy meadow.

丹尼尔自告奋勇去找她，"我一定会把莲找回来！"说完便飞奔出去寻找莲留下的气味。

不久他找到莲在绿茵茵的草地上散步。

But Lin didn't see an animal rushing towards her in the tall brush!

Daniel bolted ahead to warn her, but remembered he was to keep his mouth shut.

但莲没有察觉在高高的树丛里，
有一只动物正冲向她走来。

丹尼尔猝跑上前想警告她，
但他记得要闭嘴不可乱吠。

The animal darted in front of Lin who jumped in surprise.

"Oh it's only a rabbit!" Lin gushed, and Daniel was relieved.

那只动物蹦跳到莲面前致令她吓了一惊！

莲冲口而出叫道："噢！他不过是一只 小兔罢了！"丹尼尔也就松了一口气。

However the rabbit looked very worried and bounded away.

Then Daniel turned and saw a much larger animal following close behind!

然而这小兔显得很害怕地跃跳而去。

丹尼尔转身望去，看到一只更大的动物在后愈追愈近。

The beast had bright orange stripes, long whiskers, and a furry tail.

Startled to see someone in its path, it roared and bared its sharp teeth and claws.

这只猛兽有鲜橙的条纹，
细长的须须和毛茸茸的尾巴。

赫然遇到去路被人所挡，
他便张牙舞爪怒吼起来。

The tiger terrified both Lin and Daniel.

But then Daniel raced to Lin's side and barked, **"Bow wow! Bow wow!"**

莲和丹尼尔都被老虎吓怕了。

但这时丹尼尔跑却到莲的身旁，并吠着："汪汪！汪汪！"

Just then Lin's parents and Mama and Papa came out of the forest shouting.

It had gotten too noisy, so the tiger shrugged his shoulders and continued on his way.

莲的父母以及狗爸爸和狗妈妈从树林衝出来紧接着大叫。

那叫闹太吵了，所以老虎耸耸肩就离开他们继续上路。

Lin and Daniel leapt into the arms of their parents.

"Daniel saved me," beamed Lin, and everyone knew Daniel had been very brave.

莲和丹尼尔跳进他们父母的怀抱！

“丹尼尔救了我。”莲的脸上泛起了笑容。每个人都知道丹尼尔的英勇表现。

Back at home, everyone was glad to be safe and sound.

Hearing Daniel's bark was music to Mama and Papa's ears.

回到家中，大家都庆幸可以安然返家。

在狗爸爸和狗妈妈的耳裏，听到丹尼尔的吠声就好像听到音乐一样。

Lin kissed Daniel, “You are my best friend in the whole wide world.”

And they all agreed it was a wonderful Year of the Dog.

莲亲着丹尼尔说：“在全世界里，
你就是我最好的朋友。”

最后大家都同意这是一个美好的狗年。

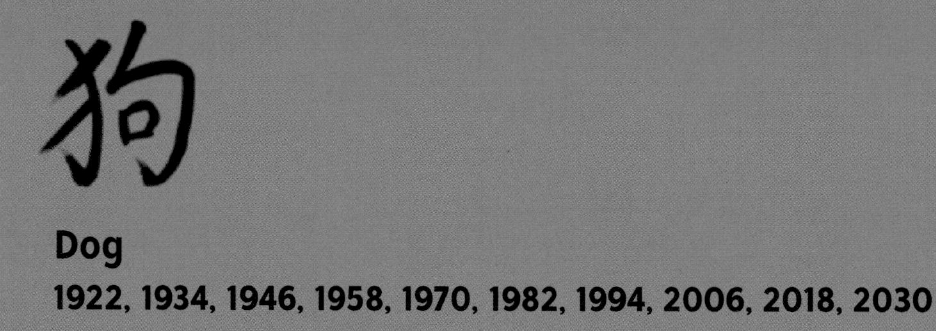

Dog

1922, 1934, 1946, 1958, 1970, 1982, 1994, 2006, 2018, 2030

People born in the Year of the Dog are honest, loyal, and faithful. They are trustworthy, good listeners, and family-loving. But they can be blunt, stubborn, and quick to snap out at others. Though it may take time to get to know them, dogs are friends for life!

在狗年出生的人士，性格老实、忠诚、可靠。他们值得信赖，是一个好的聆听者和爱護家庭，他们也许会耿直、固执及容易得罪他人，因此需要花点时间才会认识他们，知道狗是生命之友！